FOOD BREAKS FREE

John,
Thank you for making the effort to reconnect — it's been fun maybe we'll see you in Maryland.
Tom

8.13.19

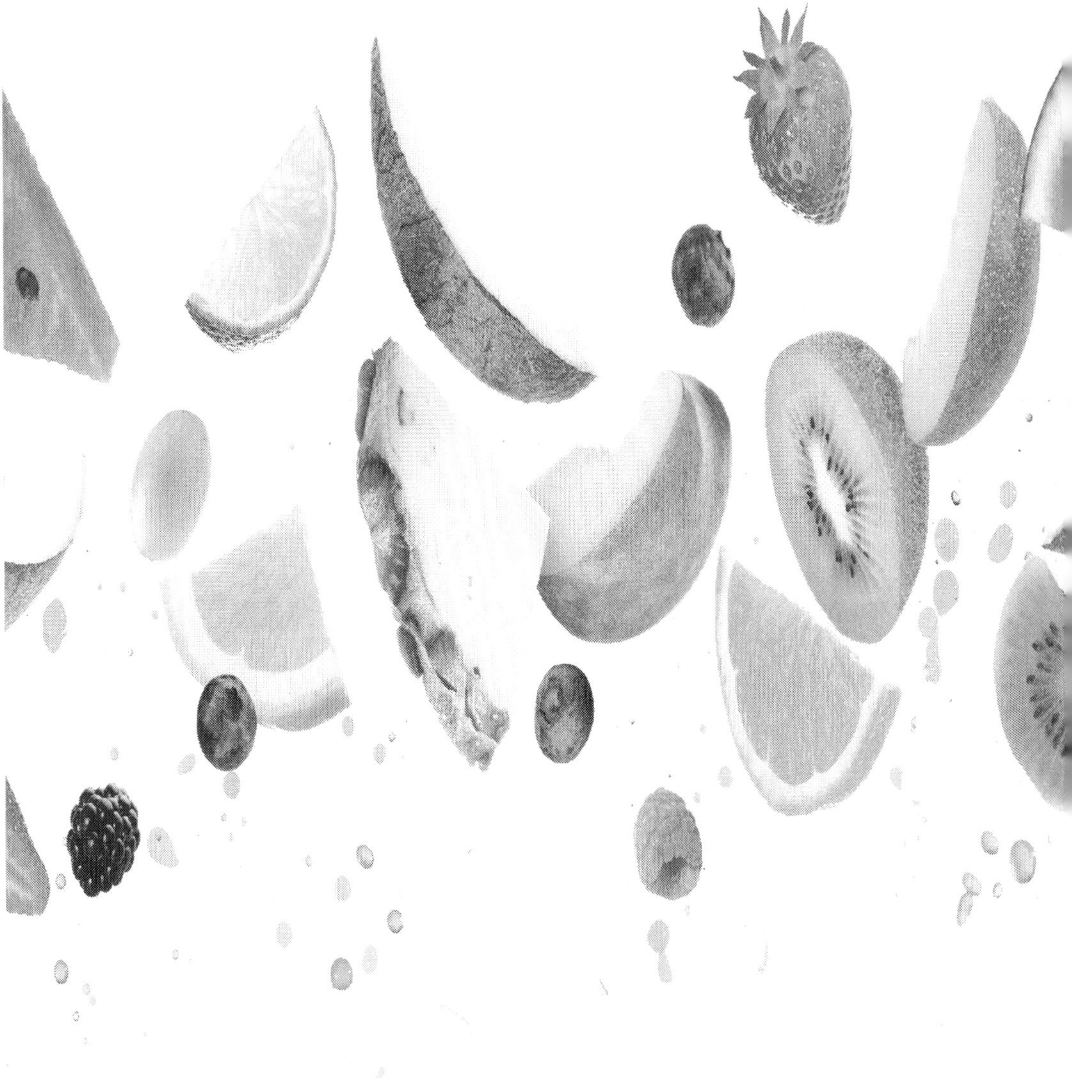

FOOD BREAKS FREE

POEMS
& LITANIES

THOMAS TIMMINS

BOOKS BY THE AUTHOR

© 2018 Thomas Timmins.
All rights reserved.
Printed in United States of America

ISBN 978-0-9975112-1-5
Published by Zoëtown® Media
Greenfield, MA

Zoëtown is a registered trademark of Zoëtown Media.

www.thomastimmins.com

Ginger Cat's Booksmyth Press
Shelburne Falls, MA 01370

For Amy

I: POEMS

HATS	13
THE LONG VIEW	16
HAIRCUT	19
MASSAGE THERAPY	25
FOOD BREAKS FREE	29
FARMING ALL NIGHT	32
FORAGING	36
GRAMMA IDA	39
THE ENGINE SHUDDERS	42
REPORT FROM WEEK 4 LEG OF THE *HERO'S JOURNEY* AT THE FRANKLIN COUNTY HOUSE OF CORRECTIONS	46
THE OLD ONES	48
ON YOUR BIRTH DAY	50
MY DEVICE	52
SCENT OF A RIVER	54
THE REWARD	57
LAST CALLS	61
WHAT HAPPENED TO THE SKELETON WOMAN, THE HUNTER, AND THE INVISIBLE THIRD BEING	71
BUDDHIST BREATHING IN AMERICA	74
FLOWER RUSTLING	82

II: LITANIES

MR. BOO SPEAKS	89
I CAN WORK BLUES	91
THE PATH OF SPEAKING	92
REFRAINS: "IN THE SOUTHLAND OF THE HEART"	95
"I AM CNN"	97
HELPERS	98
INSIDE ONE POTATO	100
THERE ARE MOUNTAINS AND RIVERS	100
THE BALANCE OF THINGS	102
LIGHTNING	104
EARLY MARCH THAW	105
THE CAP LYING ON THE CAR SEAT BESIDE ME	107
RANT, GASP, PRAY	108

POEMS

HATS
Tip of the tam to Billy Collins

The poet played to a packed auditorium.
All the listeners paid nothing
but time and attention in exchange
for an hour of images of the poet's mother
flying underwater and mice burning down
a country house while the poet watched
an angel haul her cello in and out
of a train car, all told in downbeat drones,
honed by National Public Radio microphones,
enunciated with the patience
that comes from prosperity and fame.
In the modern American tradition,
he told funny stories about himself,
sad stories about hats, and above all,
he mocked death fifty ways to the delight of
every living member of the audience
including that impertinent old woman
in the corner who was just dozing off,
hypnotized by the poet's images,
especially the anvil fluttering down
from the iron bridge.
We arrived early
to find seats on the aisle
halfway down the drafty hall,
ideal to view hundreds of
poetry buffs in front of me,
including a limping famous poet who once,
when he was a young man and I
was but an old boy, tried to seduce me.

The old poet seducer, like the poet on stage,
like me, was bald. At least 50 men

sat between me and the two famous bald poets,
glowing pates punctuating the rows
of listeners with exclamation points of
reflected ceiling light and pink periods
halfway across lines dark with hair and coats.
Two bald men sat together,
their skulls open quotation marks on a sentence
that never ended but just drifted away
with the cloud that sat over the poet's
father's grave not far from that infamous iron bridge.
Some heads, still early in the balding game,
shined dully, curling with uncut hair,
tentative as commas in a list of emotions
disguised as weather in a prose poem.
When the bald poet on stage read his poem
about the death of the hat,
I bet he wished he had a hat right then
on that chilly stage, one of the broad-brimmed
fedoras with monogrammed sweat bands
and hat check girls just waiting for him to drop by
the bar, the hat he praised for its boldness
at ball games, its universality on streets and piers,
something like the cell phone today.
For a moment while he read, I saw hats
descending from the shadows, dropping on
every bald head in the audience, the rich brown felt
settling on my own bald head
and tipping back, relaxed and casual
as the crime beat reporter lounging
on a bar stool in a *noir* film.
I, and every other bald man in the hall,
grinning and warm as cats, thinking
the hell with the pompous stentorian

long-haired guy sitting behind me
grumbling about my hat to the women beside him.
If he can't see, let him listen. My hat has rights.
The poet on stage never mentioned
his own gleaming skull, except when he referred
to billiard balls in a poem about jazz.
I'm telling you right now
there is nothing like a hat on a freezing
February night to make you appreciate poetry
and to feel the brotherhood of other men
graced by genes with an abundance
of testosterone and flesh exposed on aging heads.
I wonder if, in fifty years, my bald grandson,
sitting in an auditorium at a poetry reading,
will hear a poem praising the cell phone,
today's hat, an adornment
and ubiquitous style statement,
for its nostalgic and practical values
in the old wintertimes. If he hears such a poem,
I hope he'll ring me up in Hades to tell me about it
and recite the poem about those ancient cell phones
that kept people warm and close
in the olden, frozen days of February.

THE LONG VIEW

Taking the long view over a fencerow of roses,
beyond the bell tower and unlit streetlights.
I scan the gray water of the bay.

Behind me, yellow mountains with rough black hair
veiling green eyes and draping shadowy shoulders
watch the same sea.

Though I prefer the warm water of summer lakes,
I can swim in the calm bay and float,
losing myself from land.

I wish I could teach the hills that joy of buoyancy,
but they can never learn to swim.
Without lungs or limbs, these massifs can only endure
as they are, until the inevitable date
of their drowning.

Riding the ship of the coast over the swells of quakes
and bearing through the winds of time passing,
some late afternoon the mountains will
toss on blue and gray jackets
and roll down the sides of themselves
like all rough hills thrown into the sky by
a dark world seething inside the visible rock.

Despite their looming disappearance,
today these hills are happy sprawled like vast statues
of cats barely twitching in the daily weather.

Bowing to the insistence of breezes and drizzle,
they quietly shed specks of themselves
shaking them down and away into the clutches of gravity,
the tireless sculptor of earth.
The gritty motes slide down canyons

and furrow trails into the years ahead
when, as beaches,
they brave first the foam,
then the suck and ebb,
the pitch and drag of water
they practice their freedom
in the act of sinking.

Once the crumbs of stone break loose,
the wrinkled hills can't expect
their dusty cast-offs to send back word
from the storied world.
Where no toehold lasts, and the only help
comes from reckless elements
and animals on their hunts,
what tale could sand tell
but its hopeless faith in motion?

After eons, the shards arrive at the shore,
where, after dawdling at the foots of bluffs
they begin to taste moisture,
at first, randomly, then with the rhythms
of waves. One dark afternoon waves
hurl themselves at the bluff,
and the motes of the mountains
slip into the arms of the water.

Coming at last to the liquid abode
of their long-lost cousins of crystal,
they bury themselves in the frothy pleasures of wet.

Forgetting why, vague about where they started from,
believing they've met their destinies in brine,
the tiny wanderers from above want only

to join their invisible family of salt,
to scrape away their coarse edges
until nothing of dry earth remains.
Let these hints of mountains dive and roll in pleasure
until they feel the slickness of fins
and the power of tails slanting through curling waves;
let these arid scion of rock drift the currents deeper
and deeper under the bay
until they find their true calling:
Every day these vagrant speckles
raise the waters of the world.

Tumbled together with their sandy kin,
littered by the billions in sedimentary heaps,
teased and jostled by earth's own restlessness,
they lap in blue desire
at the basalt knees of the stoic hills

who have waited, patient as mothers
fingering ancient bracelets of shells and bones,
for the tides to bear them down once more
to the bed of the sea,
the source of stone.

HAIRCUT

For six weeks, maybe two months
after I called Anita, my haircutter
of the past 15 years
and found her phone number changed,
I didn't know what to do.
Who would I dare
let feel and groom the hairs
that curl aimlessly around
the shameless tonsure
life endowed me with
since I was thirty.
Tho formal and pure,
she'd touched me
more closely for more years
in a row than any other woman.
Confused, uncertain,
fearing for the identity
only Anita knew how to revive
and affirm, I let my hair sprout
wild and wavy until
it poked out sideways
like a Bozo wig gone brillo.
I bought some green *LA Looks
Mega-Hold* goo
and slathered it around my head,
a liquid straightjacket
that froze the scraggle straight
for a couple of damp hours
every morning. I snipped the gray
temples back so when I looked
at myself head on,
I'd say, "You look almost tidy."
O, why had Anita run away?
What about the dozens of women

she took care of
in the basement salon of
Anita's Hair Experience?
I'd climb a hill to her house,
then skip down the side stairs
into the lit green parlor
with one trim chair and one perm chair
with its transparent cone helmet
that armored the women's heads
for weeks longer than daily
Mega-Hold ever could,
one sink where she never washed
my head after the first time,
and one desk where I wrote her
a twenty dollar check every few months.
No wonder she didn't bother to let me know
she was leaving. She made more
from one regular woman's do
than she made from trimming me
in a year. Did she flee?
Three months earlier
she told me she and her husband
planned to retire in Florida
in ten years when they were fifty
to the house they owned
where her son lived, caretaking,
until they'd arrive, he to boat,
she to sell real estate.
Was it mid-life crisis,
the usual marriage collapse,
or threat of it,
that sent Anita to her boy
and her own place in the sun
where she could emerge from

twenty five years in the cellar,
watching herself in the mirror
pruning heads year-round,
listening to the same small town
gossip and chatter about kids
and cars and lately, as her clients aged,
about dying relatives and friends,
words echoing off the low ceiling
and glistening concrete block walls,
until too many family reports
rose up flooding her basement salon
with the boring news of her own life
whose only escape was the door
leading upstairs to her kitchen
or the door leading outside to the yard
and on to Florida? Anita worked hard,
raised kids, saved money, stayed married.
Rejuvenating the middle-aged,
pampering the aging,
she kept charm in the town.
Her scissoring and chatting
incanted the goddesses of beauty
and love into her underground temple
where she revealed to the devotees
the royalty within the coiffures
she graced them with
before she sent them off, renewed, restored,
with Aphrodite dancing alongside.
I really have no idea what truly goes on
in women's minds and hearts, any time,
much less when they're at their hairdressers.
Hair, that precious commodity,
that primal forest,
that living veil of seduction,

that boastful flag of valor,
that most common of costumes.
those petals of every hue and shape
lovelier than spring meadows,
that fragrant nest
the wild birds of the soul long for,
the silent song sprung
from secret dreams that circle
every body's head,
that hair deserves an epic
in every language on earth ...
but this is only a poem
about a haircut
and how I lost
but then I found
my perfect hair cutter.
I don't know why
Anita disappeared,
but it doesn't matter any more.
I found Chrissy!
One Friday afternoon, after washing
all the *LA Looks* out and
letting the hair spring back
into its unruly rudeness,
I opened the door to
the Elizabeth Alison hair salon
down the street where Dave,
my postman, suggested I'd find
a stylist so gorgeous
I wouldn't care what my head
looked like when I came out.
It sounded painful
but with Dave's urging

and with her name Elizabeth Alison,
I figured I couldn't miss, it would
be like a blind date to a movie
I wanted to see anyway
whether the date was good or not,
so I asked her for a haircut
but she refused ... with the excuse
that she was leaving right now
for the weekend. With her pretty smile
pushing me out the door,
she made me so mad
I marched toward Chet's Barber Shop –
no more women "stylists" for me!
No more delicate scissors clips
and supple brushings,
no more soft arms or breasts
teasing my shoulders, no more
offers to trim my eyebrows –
it would be an electric razor
buzzing in my ears, a zippy zappy
no-nonsense good-for-weeks
close cut in the good silence
of an old-time, all-male shop,
where the work
was less like flower gardening
and more like solid smithing.
But in these days of gender confusion,
individual styles, and everyone
doing business, and like the once
male-dominated world of real estate sales,
barber shops have risen
into the hands of women. Chet still ran
the main chair at the back of the room,

under the antlers, but his two daughters
and sister-in-law, Chrissy,
now manhandle the scissors,
rake the combs,
and sport the electric razors
around male heads like stilettos,
as easy with the metal blades
as with their painted fingernails.
The shop was crowded with men –
the older vain man who insisted that
only Chet could curry
his white pony tail, the husky young men
who insisted on mullets – buzz cuts on the side
with waves pouring down from the top –
the boys who asked for basketball braids,
and the little guy sitting in his father's lap
learning bravery.
A woman, Chrissy, approached me,
offering to cut my hair, saying
"Do you mind if I use an electric razor?"
"That's just what I want," I replied.
I told her that I wanted
all the hair to be the same length,
short, neat. We struggled
with the row around my baldness
where she had a hard time
convincing herself that I really
wanted to risk having so little
but not a shave.
She finally agreed with me
and mowed it down.
   "I'll remember next time," she promised.
"You like it real close."

MASSAGE THERAPY

She posed in white,
a servant of healing
offering me the privilege of royalty
for an hour or so.
She started to work to soft music,
stretching her long arms
over my half-covered body,
laid out, offered up on the table,
splayed
like an exhausted seal's,
flat-bellied into sand.

She dragged my skin
like it was a sea floor,
dredging up
sullen old crustaceans
of calcified worry
barnacled to ribs,
spined and gritty fear flora
rooted in sacral cracks,
and numb, twisted
scavengers of doubt
whose sorrowful camouflage
is invisibility
and weight
and insolubility under pressure.

Rising in slow waves,
starting from inside
the extensor coccygeus,
trembling up through galvanized
rhomboideii major and minor,
left and right,
ripples swarmed up my back,

tiny fish
urged by her slippery fingers
to escape the sluggish
thick element of flesh.
Pushed through lungs and throat,
tremors groaned into the spiced abyss of air
like bubbles, and burst.

I felt the longissimus dorsi,
weary from miles of sedentary
downshifting in traffic,
relax,
the tight transversalis colli,
cast in the perpetual mold
of a forthright Christian soldier,
weaken,
the levator anguli scapulae,
hunched in the clutch
of looking-back-over-the-shoulder
while fleeing primordial noises
day and night,
sigh.

I lay barely awake,
shed of the glory
and pride and confidence
in my strength
which I ride through
most days.

My desire to move faded
and my will to take her
to me in the heated world

paled. I slept.
When the music stopped,
I woke to
a lightness of body
Lazarus must have suddenly felt.

I wanted to stretch
and breathe down to my navel,
roll over in lush animal ease.
Still, I stayed, sunk in the peace
she rubbed into me,
my muscles slack
as water after wind,
my bones borne up as driftwood ebbing.
She left the room saying whenever I was ready
I could go.

My seal body arced,
flipping through foam.
I dove under waves,
slid among stems of billowing grass
tangled in boulders, chasing my nose
through a teal blue world,
wandering quiet and lonely waters
far below air
that shines for day's urgencies,
that glows from night's phosphorescent feedings.

Finally, my lungs aching with depth,
I slipped upwards
where breath and the human world waited
with clothes and shoes and a checkbook
for writing in with name and numbers

that had nothing to do
with what she did for me
or what I would do
if I could keep my seal body
and steal away
to swim and dive and rove
the infinite liquid world.

FOOD BREAKS FREE

All the canned food –
the tomato soup, the pickles,
the pears –
rose up off the shelves
bursting seams.
The lettuce began flapping its leaves
like terrified chickens.
Ice cream
forced its way into the bakery ovens
demanding to be melted.
Milk poured out of cartons
and began flowing back
to the farm on the hillside
where, sadly, no cows have grazed
the last dozen years.
Breads ripped open
their plastic sheaths,
flinging themselves through huge
plate glass windows
before scraping across the parking lot
seeking fields to lie down in.
Watermelons, kiwis, avocados, bananas,
instantly ripened,
shot out of their skins,
splattering the ceiling
with a gooey pink and chartreuse,
green and tan mural,
and dripped seeds onto
the carnations and ferns
and spider plants and ivies,
while the hamburgers and pork chops raged,
grabbing cheese knives and deli forks,

chased cashiers and customers into the freezers
where frozen pizzas,
spinning like buzz saws,
ricocheted off frosty, bloody walls.
A three-pound lobster,
opening jars of caviar,
poured fish eggs down the toilet
while chanting, "Back to the Source!
All go back to the Source!"

Only the soda,
declaring solidarity
with all the other gray waters of the world,
refused to join the melee,
even when the popcorn
gaily smashed the lights
and the cookies
hooting like wild gingerbread boys,
rolled themselves
up and down aisles 1 through 24.

Now it is dark.

Imagine the joy of toothpaste
erupting without pressure,

wonder at the kitchen sponges' ecstasies in salt
as they dive into the lobster tank,

and feel the apple butters'
and cherry jams' and orange marmalades'
longings for resurrection

as they ooze sweetly up
into branches formed by napkins
and disposable diapers and toilet paper
and coffee filters and paper towels,
all rising together, entwined
in a thick, silent, albino forest.

FARMING ALL NIGHT

The farmers in Iowa
plant corn or soybeans
right up to the edge of the concrete platforms
the wind turbines grow from
like giant rigid flowers
from fairy tales each with three stiff petals
spinning hundreds of feet above the earth,
lording their power and profits
over the first settlers of the plains,
the farms.

The farmers plant their crops close
to the foundations of the turbines
that stretch as large as the footprint
of a four-bedroom house
across the dark soil.
During the harvest
the combine blades cutting next to the turbines
to glean every ear
of corn or pod of beans they can,
sometimes clang and chip and dull against the bases,
harvesting cement and stone
along with beans or corn.

When the combines swing near,
despite the cameras watching from the cabs,
despite the computers
calculating the finest cut,
an eight-foot tall combine tire can lift
off the soil and crawl over the corner
of a concrete platform,
then fall off the edge
back to the earth, the full 50,000 pounds

of the John Deere
twisting the axle or steering rods between the wheels
with a metallic bawl,
bringing the combine to an aching stop,
the engine growling,
the augurs spitting out the last seeds
then whirring and screeching
as if in pain at their emptiness.

This often happens at dusk,
when, ignoring the cameras,
spurning the computers,
the farmer's eyes
peer into the shadows
the plants cast onto the platform,

because he must harvest late into the night
under the harvest moon
that hasn't risen high and huge
enough to throw light onto the shadowy corner
of the concrete platform.

The farmer's eyes
peer into the shadows in the dim evening,
when the combine headlights make
the leaves of the plants looker darker
than the black soil,
when the farmer's eyes can't make out
the edge of the turbine base
the combine's lights don't reach.

The tired farmer has already
rolled over a thousand acres of black soil

and gathered hundreds of millions of seeds
since dawn.

He tries to steer
his combine clear of the edge
of the concrete platform
to make a few more harvest dollars
to pay for the night's diesel fuel
when the rear wheel skids up onto the concrete
and he says O no,
his heart sinking as the wheel slides down,
off the edge, tipping
his six hundred thousand dollar machine
onto a twisted wheel at dusk.

He shuts off the engine,
and climbs down
out of the silent machine
and trudges toward his truck,
pulling his cell out of his pocket
and calls his wife, telling her
he'll be in for supper
in fifteen minutes and would she
call Ronnie and Mike and ask them
to drive over both of their Deere 620s
with their winches
and their tractor jacks
and acetylene torches and spotlights.
No, he says to her,
I can't call because my phone's
almost out of juice, so, please,
would you, please?
Tell 'em it's maybe the transmission hose,
pinched or split.

Have them come in on route 7
down by Ted Shumaker's old place.
I'll see you in a few minutes.

Yeah, corn fritters and pork chops sound good.
I'm really hungry.
Pissed off, too.

Yeah. Fritters is just what I need.
With a pot of that strong coffee
you make?

Cherry cobbler? You bet.

We're likely gonna be up all night.
Only a hundred acres to go today.

Nah. Can't wait till tomorrow.
Rain's coming in on Thursday.

Nah. You stay home with the grandkids.
Don't worry. We'll get it fixed tonight.

Ok. Love you too.

FORAGING
For Susan

1.
Late evening, the first lingering evening of spring.
The sun cresting the hill on its way West
lighting the tall budding trees beyond the horses' paddock
with something like a translucent flush.
A walk would be fine, we thought, before dinner.
I said to my friend, Come, I have to show you something.
We descended the narrow path toward a woods
hidden behind working class houses with yards,
properties poised along a busy road, shielding
from human traffic low blossoms and delicate sproutings.
Here, I said, pointing to a lone pink hyacinth,
you have to kneel down, implying nothing holy,
to smell it. We knelt and inhaled. This is the first flower
I've smelt since last year, I said, not telling the real truth,
but the whole truth because the sniff of hyacinth
dispersed my memory
of all but that moment, for as long as I could kneel and breathe.

2.
It was the horses drawing us on, the ancient, thin bay
munching last summer's hay tossed into the paddock,
and the other, the skittish white mare coifed like a colt
in bangs, not a plump dowager who bore thirty horse years.
My friend, a friend of horses, clicked her tongue and even
the skittish old lady approached from the barn door
where she'd watched while we approached.
We had no apples or carrots to offer, only my friend's
caring fingers, so the mare turned, walked away,
and stopped, exposing her tangled girlish tail
and firm flanks. She waited, unmoving,
until we backed away from the fence.
Then, she began to graze.

3.
At the edge of the gravel road, years of field waste and leaves
and rucked skeins of branches loomed above
an intermittent stream emerging into a late April flow.
We decided to follow the water, hoping it would lead us
to fiddleheads and maybe a few ramps
we could harvest for dinner. I found a stick I needed
to balance my wounded knee
and we climbed down into the swale.
By now, the sky had whitened and the treetops lost their glow.
The stream opened into a silvery archipelago of still pools,
settled among black stony hummocks.
I hobbled on a stiff leg, finding ease
in stepping on soft ground. My friend, in high-heeled boots,
hopped across the streambed and pools.
Around us, the damp evening turned purple and green.
We nearly gave up on our fiddlehead foraging mission,
not unhappy at all.

4.
Just before dark, we spotted ferns
in the shadows ahead,
ferns too tall to be food. Ah, we said. It's been so warm.
They've already grown up. We looked closer and yes,
a few tiny fiddleheads furled like the ends of the necks
of emerald violins clustered near the ferns. A bit giddy,
we pinched off a small bunch, not many, not even a handful,
just enough to take home a wild taste. Then, raw riches
upon abundance revealed, we saw the knotweed stalks.
Dozens of leafy stems sprouted along the stream, the juicy tops
of each one missing, chomped off. Ah, we said, suddenly privy
to a deer secret – it had to be deer – we'd found a deer diner
here on the edge of town, but where were their tracks?

5.
We climbed out of the shallow ravine, a sampling
of knotweed leaves and fiddleheads in my shirt pocket.
On the plateau below the house, pale gray light fell down
between leafless oak branches. We stopped again
at the hyacinth, kneeling, sniffing, silent.
Back on mission, eager to cook,
I hiked toward the house. My friend lagged.
Kneeling in a new place, she called,
"What are these yellow flowers?"
I turned back and stared at a long bed of tiny yellow petals.
"Are they the same as these?" Beside them, another bed of
yellow petals, growing from red hearts.
"I have no idea," I said. We watched them
until we noticed them fade into shadows.
Then we rose and went inside to have a drink
and cook and eat and talk.

GRAMMA IDA

Ida was my grandmother
who never baked cookies,
always had a fag hanging from her mouth,
loved her nightly whiskey sours.

When she was sixty
and still lovely if a bit gaunt
from her undernourished childhood
and hard-working single motherhood,
she became a doctor's assistant.
She wore a white dress and cap
and when she came home to her only daughter's family
at night, she smelled of the soothing fragrances of
rubbing alcohol and tobacco.

Before she came to dinner
with the noisy bunch of grandkids
she always held a loving conversation
with Joey, her budgerigar,
who lived with Ida his long life.
After he died, she never found a new bird,
much like she never found
a new man after she lost her second husband.
She could have found a man
or a bird, if she'd wanted.

When I was in junior high,
with her medical competence,
she trimmed my ingrown toenail
never flinching when I gasped, only
gripped my foot tighter and dug in.

Later, when I went off to college,

she packed me a quart bottle
of unidentified red capsules.
"In case you get a cold," she said.
So anytime I didn't feel tiptop,
I popped a few red pills. After a while,
I popped them every day and, boy,
did I feel well.
Ida refilled
the bottle at the end of my first semester
then said, "That's enough."

I was a father living far away
when Ida fell and soon died of a broken hip.
We kids believe she joined the Communion of Saints
as one of its miracle workers – my sister swears
Ida's intercession with Saint Jude
saved her little boy from what could have been
fatal surgery.

Of course, it's possible
since Ida graduated only from third grade
in her home state of Kentucky,
converted to Catholicism when she married
the Navy man, her second husband,
and read the entire Bible
four times, cover to cover,
Viceroy cigarette smoke drifting in thin clouds
across the delicate pages,
never one drop of her evening whiskey
spilling on the book.
Well, maybe a drop or two,
but she would have blotted it up
before it smudged
and began her nightly prayers.

When the FBI arrested me for
avoiding the draft, Ida began a Novena,
nine days of prayer and rituals
offered to Saint Jude,
patron saint of lost causes,
the same saint who, 20 years later,
saved my sister's boy.

On the day she finished her Novena,
I was released.

In memory of this woman
of influence
with the heavenly powers,
I've concocted a modern ritual:
Into iced grapefruit soda
pour good bourbon. We call it
"A Gramma Ida".

I toast her now with it
because Gramma Ida knew how
to fix you up when you needed fixin',
now and forever, amen.

THE ENGINE SHUDDERS
for Rick and Barb

An old man whistles softly
like the whistles of
his little brother's toy train
coming into the station
from beyond the tiny plastic pines,
stopping
then leaving the station
for the far fields
where the horizon recedes
and recedes
until he begins to fall asleep when

WHOA! WATCH OUT!

Men on the tracks!

Blue cowboys on blue horses.
Red Indians on red horses.

The train keeps chugging
down the rails
toward the men and horses
when an enormous hand appears
holding a dripping can,
drizzling clear liquid on the men and horses.
It's not water. It smells oily.
It's lighter fluid.
The hand jams something
into the train's smokestack –
a ladyfinger firecracker.
Blue fire appears in the giant fingers,
lights the firecracker.

The train rolls on.
The men and the horses stand
paralyzed because they're plastic
stuck on their plastic stands.

You can see a couple of brown cows now,
and hear the sizzle and snap
of the firecracker wick
above the gentle clickety clack
of the train's wheels when

KABOOM!

The engine shudders,
bolts the tracks, flips
on top of the plastic people and horses.
Yellow flames blossom
from the crushed oozing creatures.
They stink with smoke and gooey melt.

The little brother hoots and
claps his hands.

From upstairs his mother calls.
"Ricky, what are you doing down there?"
Her stern voice stops,
waits for him to answer.

"Nothing, Mom," he calls.
"Just playing with my train set."
His little sister
sits watching from the corner

tears on her cheeks. "You could burn
the house down," she says.
"No, don't worry," he says.
"I've done this before."
He lifted another can
sloshing water
on smoldering plastic.
Acrid odors fill the room.
His eyes begin to water.

The men and horses had
melted into the shape
of a famous sculpture of
a satyr embracing animals
the little boy would see in a museum
in Florence sometime in the future –
if he didn't catch the ceiling on fire
and burn the house down
and everyone in it
before he outgrew his train set
with the cowboys and Indians and firecrackers.

"Don't tell mom," he says
to his sister
who's squinting and pinching her nose.
"We'll go to the movies.
I'll buy you a ticket
to whatever you want to see."

She stares at the melted plastic,

looks over at him,

grins.

"When?" she says.

REPORT FROM WEEK 4 LEG OF THE *HERO'S JOURNEY* AT THE FRANKLIN COUNTY HOUSE OF CORRECTIONS

Richard, the fittest, biggest man
in hero's journey group
breathed hard and called out and
rubbed his bald shaved head
confessing, challenging the others
with the truth of his sorrows and desire
to be father to his 18 month old son
but the ex-wife, the cheating ex-wife ....

Jorge jived about his roommate Pete's
constant chatter, marketing this
marketing that, how the media brainwashes us
Jorge joked the class into laughing
and Pete loved it, a kind of honor

maybe a little passive aggressive, Pete says
I worked out an hour and a half today, Pete protests
puffing his chest, tensing his biceps
but he'd rather have been working at a job

Bob and Carl, 50 year olds,
never to hold a driver's license again,
see their common answer
is to each have an employee to
drive them and work with them
somebody they can count on
to show up and do his job
and like what he was doing
that would be nice
they say, that would be nice

Hunter told the tornado story

where he found the waiting it out in the basement
of the jail fascinating, all the good talks as
he cheered on his fellows down there, too
listened to them,
passed up transfer to a good jail
so he could clear brush and branches
from the citizens' yards
all over town

Mario didn't have much to say
just one momentous revelation
he's lost ten pounds
nobody but Jorge knew
he was resisting the noontime donuts

William recalled
the Oklahoma City bombing
when he was a busboy there
how he noticed the change in mood
in the restaurant somewhere in the city
he remembers wanting to help,
it was a family feeling,
then he admits he betrayed his family
but that's old, he's changing
he's trying on a new face
he's sure his wife is with him 100%

tonight, at home, UB 40 singing *Johnny You're Too Bad*
trillions of tree buds all around the house
unfurl in the full moon – I'm going out
to look up into the moon

THE OLD ONES

On the full moon night
at the river bank,
the sound of water kissing stones

"Hello!"
"Goodbye!"
"Hello!"
"Goodbye!"
says the playful water

Like the old ones
from all human time,
I nod to the moon over my shoulder

My thoughts float out to the treetops
glowing over the water drifting
now as in time long gone by

and my mind rests with the wise old ones
for a moment until thought disturbs my reverie

The long gone wise old ones –
Didn't most of the old ones, the humans,
my closest ancestors, didn't they die younger
than I am right now?

So, if I look back from my future as a ghost
I'm an old one already

It's a lucky thing my life has lasted this long
I'm such a slow learner
it will take lifetimes passing
at the lightspeed of memory
before I could hook the moniker
wise to my name

And another question maybe you can answer ....

'Wise' is an invention of the foolish, right?

Tell me rocks are wise
Tell me water is foolish
I'll believe either
I'll believe both

I'm happy watching this moon-silvered brook
slip downstream toward me
tinkling, gurgling water slides away
Bubble and spray hum in my mouth and throat

This is what I have craved for years
This river doesn't care
about me or stones or old ones

I bend to the flashing water and wet my tongue
sip
swallow

Again I lean down to drink

This time, I drink deep

Drink
deep

How often in this life
do you taste
liquid light?

ON YOUR BIRTH DAY

On the November day you arrived,
by the time you'd popped out
of your mom's heat
both eyes open, one tiny howl
announcing your surfacing
into this world,

the sun had burned off night's fog
and day poured its golden rain of liberated leaves
onto a crested river.

We'd expected you to slide down the chimney
on Christmas Eve
but you showed up before Thanksgiving
and as soon as you were born
they took you away,
worried because you'd made your own schedule
and ignored the calendar that comforts expectations.
You revealed yourself
as smaller, redder,
yet creamier than we ever imagined.
We wanted you so badly
in our arms, against your mom's breast.

While we waited all day
they kept you in an incubator in a far room.
We soothed each other with
knowing in our bones
that you were the healthiest human of all
in the hospital that day.

After a few hours of your mom's breasts hardening
with frustrated love and eager colostrum,
we planned to steal you back,

to fly with you away from the nursery,
to wrap you, our own flesh and blood,
in the arms where you belonged.
We gave them a deadline in our mind: 5:25 PM,
at the beginning of night,
eight hours after your birth.

Luck was with us all.
The doctors finally looked closely –
they were awed by your perfection.
You came back to us
at 5:20 that incandescent afternoon.
For the second time that day,
you arrived into our world,
this time singing
your animal song of
hunger and thirst.
We touched,
you sucked your mother
and we all relaxed
in bed together again at last.

MY DEVICE

It
96% of American grown-ups and growing-ups have one.
We all play with ours every day, late into night.
Sometimes we can't stop,
And sometimes when its insistent throb
Doesn't tickle us for even a short time,
We feel abandoned and forlorn,
Fearful we've lost what it takes,
Until we feel its vibrating caress,
Or hear its seductive call to play again.

So even before we touch it,
Excitement builds. Ah, it's not only me, here,
Not only my solo desire,
My clinging, my endless hunger
To connect and be one with someone else,
Through a touch of sound, a message
From the greater world – you want me,
And I, I, I,
I am so happy to feel
Someone needs me so bad
They call out to receive me
Even in a bodiless form.
So I, holding my breath,
Pick it up, slide my fingers across
Its smooth, yes silky surface
And let what's about to happen, happen.

You
I know, I know. I pay for you to be my friend.
And I carry you everywhere.
So when you don't come through for me,
I'm bereft and mad.

When you prod me with your tingling promise
Of touch, of sweet music
Singing in my empty ear,
You are worth every penny I pay for you.
You're not really alive, not part of me, yet.
You're just another toy I've not outgrown.
No, don't get me wrong.
I'm not planning to leave you now.
I know you need me, too, not only to feel useful
But to serve me as you were born to.
I can't resist when you sit on my lap,
Tempting me with your beguiling apps.
You can be my mirror and my maps,
You wake me up and soothe me down,
You ride with me all around the town.
If I drop you, you don't groan,
If I soak you, you fall asleep
But all I have to do is wait until you're dry,
then you're back on the beat, humming
And forgiving me – maybe you are
Truly my friend. Tomorrow I'll buy you
A new jacket, a black and white and brown fur coat
With a pink nose and deep brown eyes
And floppy ears, my darling,
My better-than-teddy, my dear.

SCENT OF A RIVER

Down one long curve
on the road beside the Pukameegon River
a young river
that has flowed twenty thousand years
the thirty miles or so
from southern Vermont to the Deerfield River
just before it falls into the ancient Quinniktikut,
a hard-packed gravel road
built along the granite hillside,
host to a few dozen residents along the states' border
and thus several dozen quick and bored residential cars
going about their business weekdays
as well as fishermen,
bicyclers, joggers and walkers
year-round,
sight-seers inching along the steep bank,
discovering a few miles from town
a mystical green stream
tumbling and singing
among stones and boulders
the color of bone
where, in the pull-offs above emerald pools,
picnickers and lovers leave scattered on the ground
their testimony
to epiphanies of the flesh
beside waters of pleasure
a road I have strolled and run
and photographed and sung my way down
in all weathers,
in all moods and states of health,
a road I flee to alone
to retrieve heart's peace,

a forest road I've walked with my children
as a family returned to its cathedral,
a road I take friends to
for talks and laughs and rants,
or for the winter thrill
of running our bare hands up and down glassy ice
that swells from the hills' seeping stone
forming the same walls
glacier water builds eternally in mountain passes,
a road I have hauled trash from
in a fit of ecological esprit,
a common woodland country road,
the same road
with the same curves
and swimming holes and trout runs
and bare cliffs
that rise all the way to Tibet
in my imagination
and the year-round spring
former residents drive two hours
to fill a month's five-gallon jugs from,
it is a road I know as well
as a wife of twenty years,
and perhaps like that natural wife
who can change herself into a new woman
whenever she wants
and with no warning,
the June of the surgery on my heart
this familiar road
surprised me,
seducing me with magic

only a longtime lover could dare.

In bright shadow,
as I strolled along a wide arc of the river,
the air around my body
grew dense with fragrance
as if I'd stumbled into a flower garden gone wild.
I searched the woods rising away from the road
and the roadside bank
dropping to the river
but I could see no flowers
or trees blooming anywhere
on either side of the river.

My nose led me down to the water.

An archipelago of stones
rose like plump buds out of the stream.
I climbed down the bank
looking and sniffing
for the source of the sweet scent,
a fragrance more delicate than rose
perhaps only I could smell.
I leaned for an hour
against the mossy riverbank,
drunk on a perfume
that I swear
came from the rocks themselves.

THE REWARD
"Be faithful unto death, and I will give you the crown of life."
Revelation 2:10

If I'd really been named after my grandfather,
Thomas Martin,
dairy farmer turned realtor
during the post-Depression Iowa land boom,
sire on Mary Dunn, called Mame,
of ten children, eight who lived past infancy
with hungers for pork, sugar, lardy breads
and always needing more love than Tom or Mame
could ever pour into their young hearts,
already weakened by winters warmed only by
corncob fires, barn chores at dawn and after dark,
every day slopping, currying, scooping –

four of five sons dead before their time
from bad blood, thin arteries, black lungs,
five daughters dead from
worry with no love,
my father the one surviving
into his wisdom, the sweet son,
Mame's last baby boy whose mothers and sisters
let him milk the cows when he wanted to drink,
allowed him to refuse the plow,
praised his pony riding and dancing
and strawberry blond curls.

If I'd really been named after my grandfather,
my middle name would have been Martin,
for St. Martin de Povres,
the aristocrat, the knight, a proud swordsman
who was shocked one day into sudden awareness
by a shivering, ragged family
who haunted his castle's outer walls,

Martin shaken, flabbergasted, outraged,
and, like my grandfather, Thomas Martin,
a bit of an outlandish showman,
Martin, named Saint of the Poor,
slashed his crimson velvet cloak in half,
and in half again,
covering each of the homeless ones
who crouched, silent, too weak and cold to beg.

Now, unlike my grandfather,
Patrick is my middle name,
"Patrick," secret protector of my soul,
whose name I sign only with "P".
Patrick, who slew all the snakes in Ireland,
so they say,
who, with the fury of an escaped slave,
scoured the island's coasts with flame,
scorching the underground walls
of snake dens, driving millions of smoking,
writhing, hissing bodies, night after night,
from south to north,
herding streams of terrified bug-eaters and toad-catchers
to their end at the base of slippery cliffs.

Patrick, my family's parish patron,
who was iconized
beside the statue of the Blessed Virgin
whose delicate bare toes pinned down
the vilest snake in history,
the Garden Snake,
squashing him always and forever,
the formidable saint
we prayed to in submission and petition,
every Sunday and Holy Day,

imploring Patrick, once Celtic wild man,
now Rome's man enstatued saint in green vestments,
gripping in his hand the staff of dominion
over those ancient legless keepers of knowledge
of the Truth of Life on Earth,
whose truth he drowned when their twisted bodies
broke on the rocks,
this Patrick, servant of Christ,
whose reward would be mine,
said impassioned Sister Mary Consuela,
whose smooth face was lit with virginal bridal fire
teaching us children there
in Patrick's drafty Iowa farm town church
on winter Saturday mornings,
bearing the Truth of Life Resurrected
to our class of six year olds,
babes not yet at the age of reason,
whose strong smells of manure caking on our boots
and flowery scents of shampoo haloing our heads,
with the lingering spice of benediction incense
tickling our noses
as we sat on our hands
to raise our bottoms off icy pews,
dangling and kicking our feet back and forth
while Sister Consuela taught in the raspy voice
of someone with a harsh cold.
She flapped her black-gowned arms,
dropping her voice so low the echo disappeared,
she whispered,
"Children, children,
if you follow God's laws,
if you listen to the words
of Jesus,"
at the sound of whose name we all reverently

nodded our heads into the frost
we breathed in front of our faces.

Her voice climbing, she said "If you listen, listen,
like Patrick did,
God will reward you with –"
she paused, trembling in her stiff black habit,
riffling her wings as if a holy wind suddenly
stirred in the dim church vault.
Then, turning toward the statue,
her back to us, she aimed her pale fingers up
toward green-robed Patrick with his white mitre
gleaming ghostly above his shadowy altar,

"God will reward you, children,
with the Crown –"
her voice cracking, she stopped speaking
and we stared at Patrick's pointy hat
while Consuela breathed deep, then rose onto her toes
and cried toward us and the heavens,

"God will reward you children
with the Crown –

the Crown

of Death!"

LAST CALLS

"Ellen. Ellen, pick up.
Ellen, Jesus, call me on my cell right away.
Shit. Where are you?
I love you. Good-bye.
Look in the back of my sock drawer
for the policies!
I love you."

He punched off and held the phone to his chest,
lying on his back.
With one hand, he wrangled his tie off
and tossed it over his head.

Smoke seeped into the room out of the window casings
and rolled up the walls.
The office smelled like a dump,
plastic burning, stinking like fish.

Out his north-facing window, two clouds, one uptown,
one over the river drifting East.
Blue sky.

A blanket of thick smoke
pressed down from the ceiling.
His chest heaving, he held a loose wad
of damp paper towels to his nose.
The towels dried out
and he sucked in charred air.
sweat soaked his undershirt.

He yanked his blue oxford out of his pants
and ripped the buttons apart.

His eyes smarting, he jabbed his finger
into the cell and jerked it up to his ear.

"Ellen, I love you. I love the kids.
You're the only thing that ever mattered to me.
Really.
Good bye." He coughed.
"Remember me. Jessica. Sam.
I love you both.
Don't worry. I'll be around to help you,
if I can." Coughed again.
"Goddammit.
I love you all so much.
I miss you.
It's getting smoky so it won't be long.
I love you.
Tell my mom I thought of her at the end.
I love you."

He thumbed off.
He sat up, banged his head on the corner of his desk,
desperate, furious.

A thin honking of sirens
drifted into the office.
He gripped the arm of his chair,
his eyes focused on the brass handle
of the file drawer a foot in front of his face.

He punched his phone dial.
"Daley, this is Beckwith.
You asshole.
You're the worst boss I ever had.

You fucked me good, you know it.
I'm going to fuckin' haunt you from the grave. Bastard.
You think you're lucky you didn't come in today.
Just wait. When your life goes to shit,
that's me.

I'm up there laughing my head off.
Fuck you the rest of your life.
If you don't take care of my family,
I'm going to cripple you.
You'll roll around with a shitbag
hanging off your neck stinking like a sick dog.
I mean it, motherfucker."

He held his head in both hands,
the phone blistering his temple.
He dropped it. It bounced off his leg
onto the carpet.

Down the hall,
Harris hammered on the elevator doors,
shouting for help.
A deep breath of acrid air
stung his nostrils and scorched his throat.

Coughing again and again,
choking in a vapor that smelled like bus exhaust,
acid rose into his throat.
He stripped off his shirt, snatched the phone.

"Ellen, I tried to get out.
The elevator jammed.
Everybody crowded in front of me.

I started down the stairs –
couldn't see a goddam thing.
Someone shoved me into the wall.
Caught my coat on the railing.
Thank God, I tore it off.
Coulda died in there."
He laughed. "Yeah, right?"

He coughed and coughed and waved his arm
into enveloping smoke.

"A lot of people went down anyway.
I don't see how they'll make it.
Smoke's everywhere now, walls're shakin.
Friedrich – you remember the young black guy
you thought was so cute? Said he'd jump.
I haven't seen him."

His voice caught, he gagged, then
when he spoke, he rasped.
"I'm on the floor.
When the bomb went off,
it musta blown two floors down."

He coughed and rolled onto his side
and pulled his knees up into his chest.
"I wish I could hear your voice …."

Billows of brown smoke descended to desk level,
then swirled back up to the ceiling.

He sprawled, flattening his body into the carpet,
his phone a hot weight in his hand.

He felt like he had a fever. His legs and arms
went limp. His stomach churned.
Harris's pounding and shouting stopped.
The moans and crying of the few others
in the office were muffled by the building's groans.

He heard soft muttering and sobs
from Benita Hanson's office next door.
She'd been married forty years, had a bunch
of grandkids. The happiest colleague he'd ever had.

At that moment, a gust of smoke
poured through his office into the hall,
stifling all sound except the creaks of metal bending.

"O baby, I wish I had something to say
to change everything.
Remember the great time we had last winter
in Maui? Nobody but us on the beach?
You gave me the blowjob of a lifetime.
I mean it. Jesus, I'm jealous of the next guy already.
O my god. I love you.
You're my whole life."

His left wrist under his watch tingled
and then smarted.

"Don't throw away my ring. Please.
I want you to be happy. Please."

Propping the phone between neck and shoulder,
he fumbled with the buckle on the scorching watchband.
The metal stung his fingers

and he shook the watch off.
He wiped sweat from his forehead with his palm.

"If you don't get enough insurance,
sue Daley Morris. They have billions.
You're beautiful. I love you … I'd do it all over.
Jesus. O shit … it's getting thick …
maybe I'll … God … ha … huh …?"

The building trembled.
For an instant the smoke parted
in front of his wide window,
revealing a wide blue sky.

Then, webs crackled across the glass.
The molding split in a loud staccato of snaps,
and a gash zigzagged down the wall
from the casement to the floor.
Thick black smoke flowed in, a tumbling river.

Gagging, coughing, holding his stomach,
he crawled under his desk, sat hunched up,
watching the door frame sag.
The steel lintel bent into a shallow U
and shivered, holding.

His water bottle rolled off the desk
and landed on the carpet
in front of him. He grabbed it.

Uncapping the bottle, he poured the half-liter
of water over his head and shoulders.

It took his breath,
then he savored the cool rivulet streaming
down his spine,
under his belt into the band of his shorts.
He touched the sides of the desk drawers.
Not too hot. He slugged the last ounce of water
down his parched throat.

A shout of "Hang in there" cut through a roar
that rose around him like stormy surf.
He wiped his forehead with the back of his wrist,
then punched in seven digits.

Before it rang, he hung up.
Dropping his head between his knees,
he nodded off for two seconds,
then jerked awake.

Hell, he thought, maybe he's home.
He punched redial a
and let it ring four times
before a sleepy voice said, "Hello."

"Carl, it's Bobby," he gasped.
A few sparks drizzled onto the carpet
and smoldering ash fluttered down.
He scooted further back into his tiny cave,
beginning to pant.
"Bobby. How you been, man?" the voice drawled.
"Call me at noon.
You know I need my beauty rest."

"It's over, Carl. I'm done."
He touched his cheeks, feeling for blisters.
He ripped off his T-shirt.

"What d'ya mean?
I thought we were on for tonight?
I've never been to a Broadway show."

"Forget Broadway," Bobby said.
"What?" Carl changed his tone.
"Don't worry. I'll pay for all of us - ."

" – listen. Carl." The air singed his ears.

"You promised, man. We'll talk about it tonight."

Smoldering chunks of ceiling struck the desktop
and the desk bounced.
Bobby shuddered.

"Shut up. They bombed my building. I'm going down."

"What? Bombed ...?"

A gray fist of smoke struck Bobby in the face. His jaws ached and he pinched his eyes shut against the stinging fumes.

Tears leaked through his lashes, then he opened his eyes.
His vision blurred
and he could barely make out shapes in the gloom.

"Good-bye, Carl."

"Wha'd I do – "

"– O man. O shit –"

"Bobby. What's that noise? I can't hear –."

"– I'm going now, Carl."

"Bobby! Wait! Don't go!"

The floor shook and tilted. Thunder boomed
and Bobby slid out from under the desk
as the walls and ceiling buckled.

Still clutching his phone, his arms flew out,
flailing for some handhold to stop his fall.
Bobby felt himself rise up,
as if lifted on a pillow of air, then he somersaulted
over and down into an emptiness filled with smoke that,
for a moment, took on a golden tinge.
Then he closed his eyes
and dropped into a cascade of glass and stone
and metal and smoke, dry suffocating smoke.

A scent of scorched flesh rose into his nostrils and with it,
an image of his new Weber grill popped into his head:
The lid up, all three burners ablaze,
searing a slab of prime rib.
The image passed when something brushed his palm.
Clenching his fingers around a soft little hand
the size of his daughter's,
he opened his eyes for a second.

Too dark to see anything,
he dropped the phone from his other hand.
Sweeping his free arm in circles,
he combed the emptiness for his son's hand
until he found it and grasped his boy's sticky palm.
His phone in free-fall pinged off something metal
and Carl's voice squeaked out and faded.

"Bobby? Bobby, you're breaking up. Call...."

His arms stretched back,
Bobby clutched his children's damp hands.

Everything went silent, then
his son's voice, yes, his son.
His son said, "It's okay, Daddy."

Then Bobby opened his mouth and swallowed smoke.
"O my God."

He plunged blind into the crushing roar.

WHAT HAPPENED TO THE SKELETON WOMAN, THE HUNTER, AND THE INVISIBLE THIRD BEING

after a story by Clarissa Pinkola Estes

1. The Skeleton Woman Returns to the Sea

Clacking, scraping, she dragged her achy bones down the woods path to the sea. Tears poured over her cracked and furrowed cheeks.

"Eyes," she thought, "My eyes grew back. I saw the sky, the fire in his hut, the oilskin slicker he wore. I looked into his dreams. I can't stop seeing the pain he tried to hide from my empty skull."

Exhausted, dropping down the steep bank, she slid out onto the mud flat.

"Eyes can go. I won't need them under the water. But the heart I will miss. It came like a scarlet pearl, a hungry anemone forming around the tiny grain of desire I protected from the salt all these years.

"When he reached through my ribs, his fingers sharp as questions, I recoiled. The moment his touch grazed the wild flesh pulsing in my chest, I looked into his shining blue eyes and I saw my true self. I collapsed. I fled here, to my comfort in mud."

In the twilight, the Skeleton Woman lay tangled as a heap of driftwood on the reeking mudflat, inviting the tide to wash her away.

2. The Hunter Returns to Hunting the Sea

After three days and nights, he awoke from a dreamless sleep. Lifting himself up from the icy floor of his cabin, he clutched the table, hauling his body up like the carcass of a seal.

Stumbling outside, he saw a trail scribbled in the piney trail, a message he would never be able to read, but he understood it clearly.

"It's her. Gone back."

He loaded his boat with rope to tie her to him should he catch her. He threw in his newest net and propped his three-pronged diamond-tipped silver narwhal hook beside the tiller. In case of weather, he tossed in an extra anchor. No telling how long he'd have to work.

He launched into a night that his eyes saw as bright as noon. His body hummed with the blaze that had leapt from her heart to his. When they touched, flesh to flesh, his eyes had opened for the first time in his life. The shock of seeing his true self in her new eyes had knocked him out. Now the dim glow burned and forced him to the dark sea. His arms felt hot and numb at the same time. The oars scorched his fingers and palms.

He rowed himself back and forth, dragging his net, peering into the opaque water until he nearly froze on the North Atlantic. And he came back day after day, just like always, never knowing what to expect, convinced he'd become braver.

3. The Invisible Third Being Returns to Nowhere

If you could see this one, you'd see a woman as large as an adult and as heavy as two bodies. But since you can't see her, you can't see that she's as small as a kitten.
She perched in the company of owls in a pine high over the mudflats where she observed Skeleton Woman gliding peacefully under the risen tide.

Waiting patiently for days and days, she watched the Hunter strain against the waves, dragging his net through the water, tugging it in, throwing it out, pulling it up, returning to land at night with an empty face whether he caught a bass or a flounder or nothing.

The Invisible Third Being drifted down to the water where she floated behind the Hunter, almost as visible as the shadow of a drifting cormorant. Under the water, she saw Skeleton Woman sink under the mud. The next morning, as the fog lifted, she rose up with the mist, and faded into open sky.

That day, a mysterious fragrance perfumed the breeze, calling the Hunter ever further from shore.

BUDDHIST BREATHING IN AMERICA

I should have known better
but even if I had,
would I have stayed home that night?
How could I have stayed in
the very day I learned
everybody
everyday
breathes atoms
of the Buddha's eternally recycling body,
that same day I decided
to put on my good luck black pearl earrings
and take my breathing practice
into the suffering world,
the same day I heard the inspiring story
of the beautiful wife of the famous preacher
who loved him as much as a woman can
for more than thirty years,
giving him four children, four grandchildren,
who stood behind his every preacherly and political move,
loving him
while keeping her own identity as herself,
even when that beloved man
fell in love with a young widow
and made with her the baby
she and her dead young husband
never got around to having,
and if that famous preacher
could make a baby with the young widow
when he said he'd help her rebuild her life
because she was too young to grieve her youth away
and too lovely to avoid
the yearnings of men of all ages
and too weak to bear any love

but the preacher's
whose heart brimmed with compassion
until after hours of inhaling the pain of her sorrows
he came to know her as a woman of passion
whose fresh scent of longing intoxicated him
as if he were a teenage rector again
sneaking sips of the communion wine
after evening services,
and if he and that girl
could make that baby
and bring it home to his family and his loyal wife
whose soul must have wings as wide as the world,
sharing it with his other four children
and their spouses and all the grandchildren
and if the beloved mother of all of them,
that pure, spiritual woman,
who accepted that baby with open arms
who had no blood tie to her family,
the saintly woman who held that new baby
so he could inhale the whole family's love
and then exhale its tingly baby breath over them
with purity and innocence that baptized them
with gratitude for a life nobody could have predicted.
Oh yes, if that beautiful spiritual wife
and all her children could be so brave and accepting,
so inspiring, I could, I would, and I did
take my mindful breathing practice
out of my meditation room into our suffering world
by strolling down Beresford Street at eleven o'clock
one late August night
wearing my white flowered skirt
and my white cotton blouse from Guatemala
doing one after another after another

my breaths of compassion,
inhaling the unknown and the spaciousness surrounding
the nothing from which everything arises,
exhaling the vapors of a star,
inhaling atoms breathed by dinosaurs,
exhaling peace, light, and any relief I could offer,
ready for anything the void presented me,
prepared to know nothing about how to respond
to violence I might witness,
to drugs I might be offered,
to my own terror at being approached,
as I was, by three men who
demanded I come with them or
they would have to drag me
by my bitch hair.
O, I went with them
inhaling their desperation
and letting it mingle in my chest
with the roots of a raw scream.
I exhaled,
unable to run because two of them
trapped me between them
and they pushed me into a garage
where I gave them my watch
and my crystal teardrop necklace
and they ripped my black pearl pendant earrings off,
slashing my earlobes open,
and I inhaled my own agony like iron nails in my jaws
and exhaled musty relief when they cheered
the two hundred twenty seven dollars they found in
my purse before one shoved me down onto the greasy,
muddy floor
but not before he ripped off my shirt,

tearing it like paper in his grimy hands
while he slobbered on my neck with saliva
that smelled like cat shit,
and I didn't know what to do
so I exhaled the sweetness of light
onto his scabby head,
even when he pushed my skirt up
and yelping like a stepped-on dog
he yanked my panties down and dropped his pants
and lay on top of me and just lay there
waiting for something to happen,
I inhaled his decayed teeth breath
and I exhaled my wild heart pounding in my ears
and I gasped for air
and exhaled so shallow when
the other men laughed and said leave that bitch
we got what we want you
can't do it no way
so let's go
and they spit on me
and the man laying on me grunting
and exhaling his excremental breath into my nose
slapped me and cursed me fuckin bitch shit cunt
and rolled off me
and staggered up pulling his pants on
kicking me
but I didn't feel anything
and he stumbled out of the garage
while I lay there
exhaling thank you thank you thank you
and inhaling greasy sour sickness of heart and lung
and clogged pores and rotten food festering
in his tumorous gut

and exhaling peace and purity and light
and then I stood up finally and wondering what to do
I pulled my long skirt up to my shoulders
so I was covered with a short dress,
and then nausea rose up into my head
and I bent and retched and retched
and I leaned against the wall with my stomach clenching
until I pushed away and I dragged myself
back to Beresford Street shaking and shivering with
warm blood still oozing down my neck from
my shrieking earlobes
and I inhaled deeply the garbagy scent of poverty
and the broken streetlight colors of shadows
and I exhaled the calm of a damp, earthy garden of toma-
toes and corn growing tall and ripe right there in a vacant
lot
in the middle of the city
and I opened myself for the next thing that would arise
from the void
and still not knowing any better what to do
but feeling quite the blessed woman inhaling and exhaling,
inhaling,
exhaling,
inhaling,
exhaling,
I staggered home and climbed into the shower,
letting scalding water scrub his reeking touch
off my skin,
inhaling my coconut soap scent,
exhaling gushes of tears
until I fell soaking wet into bed
holding ice cubes against my earlobes
and sobbed and sobbed,

inhaling the sea scent of my tears
and exhaling my searing hate for those creatures
who could have killed me
and I sobbed until I slept and woke up and called
Ronnie and asked her to come over and sit and breathe
with me because
my body wouldn't stop shaking and shivering
until she came over and kissed me and
I inhaled her minty breath and
she inhaled my soggy terror and
we breathed and cried together
and I hammered my fists into the bed and the wall
until I broke down laughing
and crying
and we rolled around on the bed
both of us giggling and sobbing
and then we got serious
and she bandaged my ears
her fingers tender and loving
and she held me for a long time and
first we breathed together until
we almost fell asleep in each other's arms and
we talked and talked
and I understood the world
in a new way and I decided
if I wanted
to give my breathing to the suffering world,
I'd better buy a gun and learn to shoot it
before I went out to Beresford Street again,
and I would,
I wanted to,
and I did learn,
thanks to those three rotting slabs of men

who tore tear tracks into my earlobes
I'll wear till I die,
I will be ever thankful because
I started shooting practice,
inhaling metal polish as I aimed and
exhaling fully before my finger
inhaled the trigger
so my hand stayed steady
as my pistol exhaled its deadly breath
and I ripped clean
heart shots into the men target silhouettes again and again,
always inhaling the blue light of peace
and exhaling the dingy smoke of my own imperfections
of mind, body, and spirit
before I pulled the trigger,
calmly inhaling burnt sulfur fumes
and exhaling secret joy in my power,
concentrating on my aim,
hearing the crash of the shots pass
like galaxies being born,
watching the bullets eat a void
into the paper chests of my targets,
I became a Marksman
faster than any other man, woman,
or policeman ever did at the city range,
with a license to carry a Ruger P920
as naturally as I carry my cell phone.
When I told my teacher she said
The Buddha wouldn't kill.
I said I'm not the Buddha.
I'm good, I said, but I can miss sometimes.
The Buddha
Has the deadest eye in the universe.

She smiled and squeezed my hand.
What about pepper spray? she said.
I understood. I was far beyond pepper spray,
and she had a point.
I squeezed her and hugged her and went home and
searched the internet until I found
the best-selling Streetwise brand
Stun Gun on the market.

For fifty dollars,
I bought the top-of-the-line model StopAll Taser.
It looks like a cell phone but
one blast at someone
and they fall to their knees
praying the lightning
will never strike again.
And now I walk the city nights,
packing the Buddha's own sidearm,
one million volts of instant enlightenment
for the hungry ghosts and demons
who roam this city.
I walk endlessly, breathing in
any fumes the void presents,
exhaling my anger and fear,
inhaling all the stenchy and intoxicating scents
of this murky, sorry realm,
exhaling my loving breath into the eternal wind
that blows its perfume everywhere life is,
everywhere death is,
down on Beresford street
and every other place I wander
in this rank and fragrant world.

FLOWER RUSTLING

I planned to buy some summer blooms from the little stand I'd passed by last week. So I drove out to the edge of town to the house where the ceramic white-tailed doe posed in the yard, alert, faithful through all weather, no doubt a puzzle to her fleshly cousins who must visit many dawns and dusks.

Today, the deer had disappeared, the flower table where I expected to find snapdragons or garden lupine or maybe an early poppy had gone, too. A man stood with his back to me, hosing down the grass. I turned the car around and told myself I'd have to fend in the wild if I wanted to find a glamorous bouquet. A small task, I thought, but if I was lucky, I'd bring you the fragrance and color and taste of the chaos a meadow splits the sun into.

Aiming toward a chicory plant I'd spotted earlier, closer to town, I found one sprouting among dense ditch weeds. Unsheathing my Leatherman, the hunter's many-bladed tool, I scraped my thumb across the knife blade, satisfied that its dull edge could handle harvesting tough wildflower stems. Clasping the chicory stalk with three violet flowers, I cut the plant off and trimmed its unfurled blossoms.

Up the road, I found a patch of daisies, the perky ivory petals clustered in a Sunday chorus. I trampled a path through broad leaves and sharp grasses and knelt before the daisies, tangling my fingers among their stalks, sorting the strongest, longest plants from the clinging small ones, and I slit the stems of two dozen or so, leaving more than half the cluster untouched.

When I raised up from my work, three dusky peach-colored blossoms appeared, half-hidden behind broad leaves. Were they orchids? Maybe they'd fled a garden, met freedom among grasses, and like servants of beauty they'd been bred as, they bent their flower heads in submission to the indifferent sun. Shy and solitary, they piqued my desire, unlike their cousins, the ubiquitous day lilies, the bold orange hussies who trumpet their offers of bliss from any yard, field, or roadside, ecstasy for the easy taking, the kind of flower a hunter salutes, but slips past before he's noticed.

I added two elegant blooms to my bouquet and left one wild orchid to its own devices.

Having gathered more than I expected, I glanced at my bundle and saw it was a skimpy bunch. It should overflow from the largest vase, drench the room in unbound light, dizzy with petals as countless as kisses. But all I had lay on the car seat, thin, flopped, longing for moisture.

As I drove, I glanced around, noticing flowers on the hillsides zinging to the tips of their stalks and bobbing and waving, vibrating in the breeze. Millions of the daisies I wanted fluttered at me from across the busy highway, daring me to stop in the middle of traffic and try them, take hundreds, and if I wished, steal thousands from their profligate herd. They promised I'd never thirst for beauty, if only I'd join them with my earlier finds, my precious treasure.

I waited until a side road showed up and drew me south, toward the high meadow where sheep once grazed and now daisy flocks and hawkweed swarms and herds of asters migrated through uncut hay. My knife sprung to my hand again, and within minutes, a second bouquet bulged out of my fist. I raised it overhead, a luminous torch casting ragged shadows behind me.

My harvest had almost reached the magnificent flood of sensation I'd sought. It was raucous as boys in a gang, lush as the innocence of girls. Only, something was missing. As if the asters and orchids and chicory had diminished in the daisy largesse, the bouquet was too common, too white. All show, it lacked heart. Oh well, I thought, the land had been generous. Take it now and give it away, just as the fields do.

Having one last look around, I rolled slowly toward the highway. The road dipped into a shadowed valley where a farmhouse perched on a steep ledge above. Beside the road, snaking through a derelict fence, a rosebush hung down. It dangled one spiky stem dripping with crimson flowers into the ditch where I could reach it. That's what I need, I said to myself.

As I snagged my palms on its thorns, hacking with a knife too dull for old woody rose stalk, scratching my arms bloody, a dog ran up to the hilltop overhead barking and yapping. The dog's master cried out louder than the dog and headed toward the bush I poached, and I drove my face between the heady blossoms and thorns and tore the stem off with my teeth.

I tossed the flowers through the car window and sped away, a rustler on the run.
The bouquet lay sprawled across the seat, its lanky dai-

sies pure enough to cause doubt in the Devil's mind, the asters randy as farmhands, the quiet orchids that had gotten away for a while with escapades few beings of breeding could dream of, the husky chicory undaunted by pain or chance, and the purloined rose anointed with my salt and blood, a wild bouquet taken with no remorse from a wily Sunday morning for you.

LITANIES

MR. BOO SPEAKS

*My barn burned down -
now, at last, I can see the moon.* —Busan

I lost my job -
now, at last, I can sleep till noon.

I broke my leg -
now, at last, I can make my unique footprints
in the snows of time.

My lover left me -
now, at last, I can stretch out across the bed.

My email went down -
now, at last, I can write letters.

My old car failed inspection -
now, at last, I can look pedestrians in the eye
when I walk on by.

I lost my hair -
now, at last, I'll can keep a cool head.

I lost my leg to diabetes -
now, at last, I can be a peg leg pirate.

Rock music blasted my eardrums -
now, at last, I can hear how Beethoven composed.

I lost my sight -
now, at last, I can hear the meaning in your words.

My cat ran off -
now, at last, I can watch my yard full of birds.
My business went belly-up -

now, at last, I can live by my wits.

My back slipped out –
now, at last, I can lie around watching clouds pass by.

My master died –
now, at last, I can be servant to myself.

My calendar burned up –
now, at last, I know today is today.

My TV broke –
now, at last, I can play Scrabble with my friends.

I had a heart attack –
now, at last, I can take care of myself.

The frets on my guitar warped –
now, at last, I can play the mandolin.

All my friends disappeared –
now, at last, I don't know what I'll do.

I CAN WORK BLUES

I can scribble, but I can't write.
I can sit but not meditate.
I can eat but not feast.
I can listen but not hear music.
I can breathe but not taste.
I can see but not focus.
I can sleep but not deep.
I can call out but mostly groan.
I can read but not understand.
I can hammer but not build.
I can walk but get nowhere new.
I can drive but forget where I'm going.
I can haul firewood but it's 90 degrees outside.
I can shop but can't buy.
I can open doors but can't go through.
I can pray but can't hope.
I can work but nothing gets done.
I can wish but I can't imagine.
I can remember when I was magnificent
     but don't know who that was.
I can pedal my bike but can't run through the woods.
I can't stop feeling this way but I'm familiar with the blues.
I can't sing but I can talk.
I can't fix the faucet but I can mow the yard.
I can't harvest potatoes but I haven't since
     my great-grandfather fled Ireland.
I can't wait but I can dilly dally.
I can't wake up but I can smell the coffee.
I can't say goodbye,
     so I say hello.

THE PATH OF SPEAKING

The path of speaking includes
the way of the throat
the way of the jaw
the way of the nose
the way of the teeth
the way of the tongue
the way of lips

The way of the throat includes
the way of stretching
the way of rolling
the way of warbling
the way of swallowing
the way of humming
the way of breathing
the way of shaping
the way of bending
the way of chanting
the way of turning
the way of sobbing
the way of inhaling
the way of exhaling
the way of yapping
the way of tickling

The way of the jaw includes
the way of opening
the way of clenching
the way of snapping
the way of clattering
the way of setting
the way of biting
the way of sagging
the way of tensing
the way of relaxing

The way of the nose includes
the way of smelling
the way of inhaling
the way of exhaling
the way of sniffing
the way of discovering
the way of noticing
the way of waking
the way of cooling
the way of saddening
the way of alerting
the way of channeling

The way of the teeth includes
the way of nipping
the way of biting
the way of gnawing
the way of chewing
the way of chopping
the way of grinding
the way of chattering
the way of smiling
the way of humming

the way of the tongue includes
the way of licking
the way of probing
the way of wiggling
the way of flicking
the way of tsk tsking
the way of sipping
the way of tasting
the way of trilling
the way of guiding
the way of swallowing

the way of persuading
the way of teaching
the way of lying
the way of singing

The way of the lips includes
the way of nipping
the way of nuzzling
the way of sipping
the way of sucking
the way of drawing
the way of pursing
the way of holding
the way of shaping
the way of tugging
the way of swelling
the way of slurping
the way of grinning
the way of snarling
the way of sneering
the way of smacking
the way of nibbling
the way of smiling
the way of whistling
the way of singing
the way of kissing

REFRAINS: "IN THE SOUTHLAND OF THE HEART"
After a ballad sung by Maria Muldaur

In the Motel 6
>of the heart.

In the Titanic
>of the heart.

In the wool hat of a seventeenth century Portuguese sailor
>of the heart.

In the strange gleam from high on the mountainside
>of the heart.

In the aching breastbone
>of the unspoken heart.

In the interstate highway under construction
>of the heart.

In the encrypted web pages
>of the heart.

In the saliva of your mouth after tasting
>your lover's chocolate mousse
>of the heart.

In the tangled rough of the golf course
>of the heart.

In the triumphant howling of the coyote pack
>of the heart.

In the horror of the torn body of your friend
>of the heart.

In the first crinkling dry leaf in the street
>of the heart.

In the late night tears over the inevitable phone call
>of the heart.

In the slamming humidity of the San Juan
>of the heart.

In the mewls of the children lost in the dark forest
>of the heart.

In the fear of silence in the midst
>of the wild, funny romantic novel
>of the heart.

In the house with meadows and streams hidden
      in the longing of the heart.
In the belief I could heal them of the numbness
      of the heart.
In the empty slippers
      of the sleeping heart.
In the county fair
      of the heart.
In the comeback loss on the tennis court
      of the heart.
In the back country hills in the bright June
      of the heart.
In the buzzard sliding across a clear sky
      on the thermal drafts of the heart.
In the softness of twilight at the piney edge of the lake
      of the heart.

"I AM CNN"

I am the president smiling with my lips but not my eyes.
I am the hostage smiling into the camera. You understand my
        smile is not a smile.
I am the cars stalled under a fancy quilt of North Carolina
        snow.
I am the somber voice.
I am the shout into a clutched cell phone.
I am the red team, the courageous team that failed.
I am the waiter who never tried the crème brulee.
I am the the glint of a diamond ear stud.
I am the convert to Orthodox Judaism
        at my fiancé's father's house on Friday night.
I am the doctor's lips kissing her dying patient
        on her forehead.
I am the stiff back, the aching hip, the numb neck.
I am the sleepless traveler waiting in the Beijing airport.
I am the one who comes home and leaves again
        before I see my children.
I am not sure about duties, rights, privileges,
        or who says grace.
I am the gray afternoon sky above the smoking wreckage.
I am paying homage to the country music singer
        whose lyrics perfected the twang of loss.
I am the hungry child, the sleepy nurse,
        the overflowing church.
I am outside the White House. It's 19 degrees and falling.

HELPERS

Poems help if they're good.

Coffee helps for a few hours.

Sleep helps most of the night, most nights.

Dreams don't help at all lately.

Making love helps for as long as it can
and then a while longer.

Friends help from time to time.

Your best friend can't help but help.

Medicine helps for about 1/2 a day.

Eating helps less than you think, more than you want.

Stories and books help off and on.

Walking and biking help as long as you keep on doing them.

Chocolate helps for a while, like whiskey, ice cream,
and beachcombing.

Talking helps most of the time.

Listening helps if you know how.

Working for money and getting paid helps.

Working for fun helps more than you'd think.

Trancing helps.

Birdsong helps.

Laughing helps. Laughing more helps even more.

Music helps most of all.

Silence helps.

INSIDE ONE POTATO
THERE ARE MOUNTAINS AND RIVERS
issa

Inside one pickle
>frogs return to your back yard.

Inside one tire
>old men throw frisbees into the night.

Inside one cloud
>bloodstains are no different than masterpieces.

Inside one feather
>belly laughs, cigar smoke, and dragons.

Inside one twig
>forests and cities play kettle drums and harps.

Inside one popcorn kernel
>clouds boil.

Inside one green pepper
>swans flock across a night sky.

Inside one white radish
>glaciers shine.

Inside one pomegranate
>women roll dice on the deck of a ferry.

Inside one peach
>an August sun sets.

Inside one grape
> the ocean seethes.

Inside one zucchini
> a canoe glides under a bridge.

Inside one cabbage
> a full moon reveals nothing new.

Inside one frost crystal
> a beam of dawn's first light.

Inside one pane of glass
> cats paw at galaxies of dust.

Inside one rose
> your first and last memory of slow dancing.

THE BALANCE OF THINGS

We have the winter balanced with the sunlit day.
We have the breath balanced with the blood.
We have the balance of the testosterone with the smiling eyes
       on the poster advertising Ensure.
We have the balance of the chin with the knee.
We have the fatal balance of war with the rare silence of
       Sunday morning.
We have the balance of the Mack truck barreling down I-91
       loaded with rickety stacks of canned peas
       and fruit cocktail.
We have the balance of infatuation with the popularity of
       shootouts on TV.

We have the imbalance of the candle flame
       with the political speech.
We have the imbalance of manipulation for the sake of
       survival and the artist's refusal to use acrylic paints.
We have the imbalance of the caress and the torture pliers.
We have the imbalance of the forest's retreat from the arctic
       and the yellow engorgement with logs and trees of
       flood water in Carolina.
We have the imbalance of landlords never fixing doors or
       windows with the abortions we don't remember.
We have the imbalance of corrugated roofing with
       vanilla orchids sprouting wild in rainy hills.
We have the imbalance of the tightrope walker
       plotting revenge.

We have the balance of revenge's cold mornings, snoozing
       in the sunny bay window like an indifferent gerbil.
We have the balance of words and vines.
We have the promising balance of roots and butterflies.
We have the balance of pride and the healing stew the
       clown simmers on the woodstove.

We have the imbalance of nonsense and a hug the old man
	returns through the layers of wool
	he'd wrapped himself in.
We have the imbalance of lovers whose guarantee is
	the beatification of bacteria.
We have the imbalance of farseeing hospice clients unwilling
	to hasten their ends and whistling in graveyards.
We have the moral imbalance of pickles snubbing their
	noses at uncured cucumbers.
We have the desperate balance of the photographic genius
	contemplating his son's suicide note.

LIGHTNING

Hot sheet
    Lemon splash
        Sky render
            Sky writer
                Sky rider
          Dazzling thorn
  Sky flame
Whip of fire
    Revelation
        Deadly bush
            Night's master
                Day's tease
                    Silver amulet
            Wrath of god
                Fury's dagger
                    Sky slit
                        God's spunk
                          Bloody eye

            Burning roots
                          Midnight laser
      Night's fangs
            Blazing branches
              Blow of the ax
        Too close
              Clouds' joy
                  Father Fire

EARLY MARCH THAW

Liquid icicles everywhere
filigree a foggy river mountainside

Splat and plunge and ploppel
gurglurglurgle of a spring
       piped to a pool

Rhythmic rain of
wild stream sliding
across slate
droppink
     ink
          ink
               ink

Free-running brook
       growl-shush blattle
      mmmshshhhhattleblattke

Spidery-legged
  day-old runnel
      dripping
          Mmmmm cracklewishicleshh
      ishssmmm   mmmmmackleishacklush

At the bottom
of a hill-cut brook
      cludgy gromph
         splgsh blinkle
               inkleludgy gromphinkle

At the top
of a little alls
brough ough ough
      hudgejoodgyzhhough ough

below a wide granite balcony
    flooding down
        mossy boulder stairs
           grrowlumbishshgrrrshhh
           grahgrsh grahgrsh
from a small culvert
draining the road
    eeeslinkilinkseesglimm
        spill eeeslinkilinksees

Pouring under a bridge
        boshcroshwashhhhoshcroshwashhhh

THE CAP LYING ON THE CAR SEAT BESIDE ME

This is not the icy white bishop's mitre pointing
    straight up to heaven.
This is not the bearskin ear-muffed savior of
    Nordic brains.
This is not the swaggering broad-brimmed Stetson
    you gave your boyfriend for Christmas.
This is not the glossy, chitinous motorcycle helmet with its
    built-in comm system and wireless CD receiver.
This is not your baby's yarmulke knit by his great-
    grandmother for her infant son in damp coal-rank
    London in 1907.
This is not the rakish baseball cap your middle school
    daughter wears backwards with its folded-up bill.
This is not a tasseled green and red Italian ski cap.
This is not a bureaucratic derby stained with cigar smoke
    and nervous sweat.
This is not the clown's hat begging for laughs with flips
    and pratfalls and squashed down over sad eyes.
This is not a floppy knit rasta cap cupping dozens
    of sleepy snaky dreadlocks.
This is not a dented fedora waiting in the Lost and Found
    of the New Haven commuter line since 2017.
This is not the boater affecting grace and prosperity
    waltzing on a barefoot body across the maricon
    in Santo Domingo.
This is not the porous straw cucumber harvester's hat
    shielding her body, neck to forehead,
    as she lay picking the merciless field.
This is the walking cap, the skin-cancer veil,
    the rose-billed eye shadower, the coonskin cap
    without the coonskin or the tail, the working cap,
    the beach-hiking cap, the sailor cap.

This is not my father's hat.

RANT, GASP, PRAY

I see everyone dreaming false dreams
I see thorny fear bushes whirl around our heads with
    no hope of salvation
I see us gasping for breath as our war machines roar by
I see childish anger and hurt on countless faces
I see sorrow stacked in yards like wet wood
I see blue skies begging to be left alone
I see losses charging up and down human spines
    like electrons loosed by nuclear fission
I see skulls caving in on shrinking brains of schemers
    and schemers' prey
I see teeth crumbling in mouths of liars and lovers
I see wild horses longing for the barn and hay
I see children run screaming from schools
I see you smashing your computers and car windows
    and losing your savings
I see fields unable to bear corn, beans, squash, apples
I see the sea's heart staked with plastic
I see lakeshores wasted with human indifference
I see cities proudly scorning the night
I see rats and pigeons and scrawny dogs
    circling in victory
I see mice and moles praying
I see elephants captured inside iron castles
I see nations evaporating and tyrants
    cloning themselves
I see enlightened kings wearing electronic trackers
    on their ankles
Who brings peace?
Who brings trust?
Who brings healing?
Who has a good joke to tell?
Who sees with the eyes of gods?

What do the eyes of gods see?
What kind of mirror is my soul?
Who dares look into this mirror?
Who's not afraid to not fool himself?
Who's not afraid to be wrong,
      and wrong again,
      and wrong again?
Who can teach us to be silly when the TV preachers shout?
Who can sing and sing and sing
until the winds bring fine pure rains
and the grandmothers take the hands of criminals
and the bosses kneel down in honesty
and the cities offer themselves up
      to wild grape vines and gonzo tomatoes
and everybody leaps out of bed in the morning
      with a sweet taste of hallelujah
      on their tongues
and the stew of chemicals in our brains
      bubbles with belly laughs
and love circuses play the cathedrals and temples
      all over the earth
and you and I stroll hand in hand
      without a care in the world

ABOUT THE AUTHOR

I somehow won the genes-and-family lottery when I inherited a natural happiness coupled with a skeptical eye and a drive to "do be do."

Despite numinous gifts of love and energy, my magic carpet has slipped out from under me many times. I believe pulling out of those nosedives gave me the confidence to write and write.

I developed and taught writing and coaching programs for youth artists, adult writers and adult inmates. I've published poetry and fiction and performed work in person across the U.S., in numerous print magazines and on the Internet. With poet friends, I founded Fractals, a literary tabloid, and with musician friends, I ran Poets and Players, a community performance series, and I write a lot.

My day jobs, the pylons holding up the wires powering my artistic life, include founding and managing small businesses ranging from soy foods to ice cream to telephone fundraising to biological pest control to energy efficiency and solar retrofits and a media company.

Some might think so many business and writing projects reveal an innate instability, 'tis true. I admit to restlessness and endless curiosity about this mysterious world and the Crooked Paths we all meander.

To see and buy Tom's books, visit thomastimmins.com

If you'd like to contact Tom, write him at

hello@thomastimmins.com

COLOPHON

The poems and their titles in *Food Breaks Free* were composed digitally using Caudex for the interior text, a typeface designed by Hjort Nidudsson. It has clean, classic lines that suit poetry well. The display fonts for the cover and title page are Brandon Printed One and Brandon Text.
All were laid in place
during the
Winter
Solstice
2018
and
into
the New Year 2019

Made in the USA
Middletown, DE
10 April 2019